The Vampire's Curse

Don't miss the first two spine-tingling
Secrets of Dripping Fang adventures!

ℳ S E C R E T S   O F ℳ

DRIPPING FANG

BOOK ONE:
The Onts

BOOK TWO:
Treachery and Betrayal at Jolly Days

SECRETS OF
DRIPPING FANG

BOOK THREE

The Vampire's Curse

DAN GREENBURG

Illustrations by SCOTT M. FISCHER

HARCOURT, INC.

Orlando Austin New York San Diego Toronto London

*I want to thank my editor, Allyn Johnston, for her macabre yet soulful
sense of humor, for her eagerness to explore ideas beyond the bounds of taste,
for understanding an author's poignant thirst for praise, and for helping
me say exactly what I'm trying to say, except more gooder.
I also want to thank Scott M. Fischer,
an artist with dizzying technical abilities and a demented genius
at combining terror and humor in the same illustration.*
—D. G.

www.HarcourtBooks.com

Library of Congress Cataloging-in-Publication Data
Greenburg, Dan.
Secrets of Dripping Fang, book three: The vampire's curse/
Dan Greenburg; [illustrated by Scott M. Fischer].
p. cm.
Summary: Having been reunited with their zombie father only
to have him turn into a vampire after drinking an experimental
elixir of life, the ten-year-old Shluffmuffin twins continue to try
to elude the giant ants who want to enslave all humans.
[1. Twins—Fiction. 2. Brothers and sisters—Fiction.
3. Ants—Fiction. 4. Vampires—Fiction. 5. Cincinnati (Ohio)—Fiction.]
I. Title: Vampire's curse. II. Fischer, Scott M., ill. III. Title.
PZ7.G8278Sec 2006
[Fic]—dc22 2005013710
ISBN-13: 978-0-15-205469-4 ISBN-10: 0-15-205469-3

Text set in Meridien
Designed by Linda Lockowitz

First edition
A C E G H F D B

Printed in the United States of America

For Judith and Zack
with spooky love

—D. G.

Contents

The Vampire's Curse

CHAPTER 1

Can Dad Come Inside and Play?

"Zombies . . . zombies . . . zombies . . . ," said Cheyenne, thumbing through the encyclopedia under *Z*. "Okay, Wally, here we are. '*Zombie:* a member of the walking dead, usually the result of a voodoo curse; zombies are found chiefly in the islands of the West Indies and, sometimes, Cincinnati.'"

"'Zombie *Cures,*'" said Wally excitedly, reading over her shoulder. His excitement faded as he read the next sentence: "'There are at present no known cures for zombiism.' Darn!"

"Darn!" echoed Cheyenne.

When the zombie outside Professor Spydelle's

house in Dripping Fang Forest had turned out to be their father, Wally and Cheyenne Shluffmuffin were pretty surprised. Dad had drowned in a Porta Potti accident at the Cincinnati circus three years before, so they assumed he was dead. Now here he was again. But since he was a zombie, he was still technically dead. The encyclopedia said there were no cures for zombiism, so Wally and Cheyenne didn't know what else they could do for him.

Wally was ready to give up, but Cheyenne wasn't discouraged.

Although Wally and Cheyenne Shluffmuffin were twins, their outlooks were quite different. Cheyenne saw only the good side of life, Wally only the bad. Cheyenne saw ice cream and thought sweet frosty deliciousness. Wally saw ice cream and thought sticky hands and spots on your shirt that won't come out in the laundry.

Professor Spydelle came into the family room, puffing on his pipe—a sweet smoky smell.

"Ah, there you are, children," he said in his

dignified British accent. "Did you bring in more firewood?"

"Not yet," said Wally. "Professor Spydelle, we need to ask you a favor. A big one."

"Why, certainly, Wally," said the professor. "What is it?" He sank into one of the net hammocks that stretched across the Spydelle living room. His joints creaked as he settled down.

"Somebody we know sort of well is outside," said Wally. "He looks kind of gross, but if you don't mind, we'd like to bring him inside."

"Who is this person?" asked the professor with a kindly smile.

"Our father," said Cheyenne.

"Your *father*?" He frowned. "I don't understand. I thought you children were orphans."

"We *are* orphans," said Wally. "Dad is dead."

"Great heavens!" cried the professor, hopping out of his hammock. "Let me help you with the body."

"Oh, you don't need to," said Cheyenne. "Dad isn't exactly a body yet. He's just kind of staggering around out there. He seems to have become a zombie."

"A zombie? My word! How fascinating! Let's go out and have a look at him."

Professor Spydelle followed the Shluffmuffin twins outside. Zombie Dad stood in the front yard, muttering to himself. Hanging from his body were pieces of rotting skin. You could smell him from clear across the yard, the sickly sweet odor of bloated roadkill before it explodes.

"Shy, Wa, me Da," he muttered.

The professor was as thrilled as a kid with a new puppy.

"It *is* a zombie!" cried the professor. "This is extraordinary! I mean, of course, I'm so terribly sorry for your tragic loss and all that, but, um, this is absolutely extraordinary!"

"Shy, Wa, me Da," muttered Mr. Shluffmuffin.

"Can you make out what he's saying?" asked the professor.

"Not really," said Cheyenne.

"Can you tell me how he died?"

"Sure," said Wally. "Three years ago he fell into a Porta Potti at the circus and drowned."

"Remarkable!" said the professor. "You know, children, besides voodoo curses, the only other way to become a zombie is drowning in a Porta Potti."

"Really?" said Cheyenne. "I didn't know that."

"Oh yes," said the professor. "That's a well-known scientific fact."

"Awesome," said Wally. "Hey, you wouldn't happen to know of a cure for zombiism, would you?"

"*Know* of one?" Professor Spydelle chuckled. "My dear boy, I *invented* one."

"Shy, Wa, me Da," muttered the zombie. He broke off a rib and used it to scratch an itch between his shoulder blades.

"What do you mean you invented one, Professor?"

"Years ago," said the professor, "I spent a great deal of time and money developing a special life-restoring elixir. My first efforts were a disaster, but eventually I found a way to make

6

it work. I was able to bring back to life one of the museum's deadest animals, which had been found frozen in a glacier—a saber-toothed tiger. It had been dead, oh, at least fourteen thousand years, but my Elixir of Life made it live again."

"Awesome!" said Wally. "What happened?"

"Well, unfortunately, the saber-tooth ran amuck," said the professor, looking embarrassed. "It smashed several expensive exhibits and, sadly, it also killed a night watchman."

"How awful," said Cheyenne. "What did you do?"

"Well, I had to, uh, de-animate the tiger and return it to its glass case. I didn't want to answer embarrassing questions about the tiger and the elixir. So, although I sensed it was somehow wrong of me to do so, I stuffed the night watchman, dressed him up in an animal skin, and put him in the caveman exhibit."

Zombie Dad tapped Wally on the shoulder. "Shy, Wa, me Da," he repeated.

"Just a *minute*, Dad, we're talking with the

professor here," said Wally. "Sorry, Professor. What happened next?"

"People kept asking what happened to the night watchman," said the professor. "It became quite tedious. Eventually, they stopped, though, and all went well for a time. Then one day my beloved human wife, Shirley, got bitten by a black widow spider. By nightfall she was dead."

"I don't understand," said Cheyenne. "Shirley is a giant spider herself."

"True, but she wasn't *always* one. When I first married her, she was a normal human, just like you and me. When poor Shirley died, I was devastated. My whole world collapsed without her. But then I had an idea. Using my Elixir of Life, I was able to bring her back from the dead."

"You actually brought Shirley back from the dead?" Wally asked.

"Yes," said the professor. "Unfortunately, during the process something went terribly wrong. Shirley started growing huge and hairy. She developed extra eyes. She developed extra legs. She eventually transformed into a giant spider."

"What did you do?" asked Cheyenne.

"Well, naturally, I was disappointed to find my wife had become a giant spider. But I got over it. I told her I still loved her, and we've learned to adapt to her, uh, new habits."

"What kind of new habits?" Cheyenne asked.

"Food preparation, for one thing. As a human, she used to cook food in the normal human way. As a spider, she . . . well, she injects her saliva, which turns it into a kind of mushy jelly. It's actually rather tasty once you get used to it. But then there's the problem of making babies."

"Uh, what problem is that?" asked Wally, not sure he wanted to hear the answer.

"Spiders can't make babies without killing and eating their husbands," said the professor. "So, as you can imagine—"

"SHY, WA, ME DA!" screamed Zombie Dad.

"*Okay*, Dad, *okay*," said Wally. "Professor, can we bring my father inside?"

"Of course," said the professor, "of course."

With the professor leading the way, Cheyenne and Wally brought Mr. Shluffmuffin into the house.

Shirley entered the family room from the kitchen. When she saw the zombie, she leaped straight up in fright, landing on the ceiling with all eight spidery feet, like a cat falling upward.

"Oh, sorry to startle you, my dear," said the professor, peering ceilingward. "We have a guest, the children's father." He turned to the twins. "Frightfully sorry, but I don't believe you told me his name."

"It's Sheldon," said Cheyenne. "Sheldon Shluffmuffin."

"Shirley," said the professor to the spider on the ceiling, "may I present Mr. Sheldon Shluffmuffin. Mr. Shluffmuffin, my wife, Shirley Spydelle."

"Pleased to meet you, Mr. Shluffmuffin," said Shirley from above their heads. She slowly let herself down from the ceiling on a nearly invisible silk thread.

"Shir Spy, me Da," said Zombie Dad. "Spy, you clyde uppa waaa spow?"

"What did he say?" Shirley whispered.

"I don't know. We can't understand him," said Cheyenne.

"How old a gentleman *is* he?" whispered Shirley discreetly. "Do you mind if I ask?"

"Forty-one," said Cheyenne. "But he's been dead for three years."

"Ah, I see. Well, that explains it," Shirley whispered. "I was going to ask why he didn't take better care of himself. Is he going to be, uh, staying with us for a while? I only ask because of the smell."

Cheyenne and Wally turned to the professor for an answer.

"Right," said the professor. "I thought I'd try a little of my Elixir of Life on him, Shirl. If I start mixing it up now, I could have some ready right after dinner."

"Well then, please do stay for dinner, Mr. Shluffmuffin," said Shirley.

"Me Da," said Zombie Dad.

"Do you know what he'll eat?" Shirley asked.

"Most zombies do seem to like human flesh," said the professor helpfully.

CHAPTER 2

The Professor's Elixir— Get a Life!

Because Mr. Shluffmuffin's body parts kept dropping off and falling into the gravy, dinner was less than enjoyable. The main course was Roast Turkey Stuffed with Mushy Jelly. It tasted okay as long as you didn't think too hard about how the jelly had gotten that way.

The twins politely refused the cranberry jelly till they learned it had come straight out of a can, and then they ate seven helpings of it.

Finding that none of the serving dishes contained human flesh, Zombie Dad gnawed unenthusiastically on a table leg, but otherwise showed little interest in eating. Dinner conversation with him was difficult at best.

"So, Mr. Shluffmuffin," asked the professor bravely, "what brings you to Dripping Fang Forest?"

"To Dri Pinfan For?" said Zombie Dad. "Lees womp. Lees womp, come Dri Pinfan For. Fine Shy, fine Wa. Fine me Da."

"Ah yes, quite so. Fascinating," said the professor. He turned to Cheyenne with a questioning look.

"I don't have a clue," she whispered, shrugging.

Dessert was some kind of green Jell-O, and once again the twins politely refused it till they learned it really *was* green Jell-O—and then they ate seven helpings.

When dinner was over, everybody pitched in to clear the table. Even the zombie tried to help, but he dropped every dish he picked up. Then he tripped and fell on the table, causing it to crash to the floor, smashing all the rest of the dishes to smithereens.

"Perhaps now would be a good time to take

Mr. Shluffmuffin into your lab, dear, and give him that elixir of yours," Shirley suggested.

"Excellent suggestion, my love," said the professor. "Come along then, Mr. Shluffmuffin. Come, children. I think you'll find this interesting."

Zombie Dad and the twins followed the professor into his darkened laboratory, the zombie colliding with various pieces of furniture on the way. On a long table in the lab was a row of glass flasks filled with interestingly colored liquids— red, orange, pink, turquoise, and purple. Under each flask a low blue flame was making the liquids boil and bubble and smell like farts.

"Ugh," said Wally, "what's that awful smell, Professor? Besides Dad, I mean."

"Sulfur dioxide," said Edgar. "And that's how it's *supposed* to smell."

He turned off all the flames, poured what was in the flasks into a glass beaker, then stirred the mixture. The liquid in the beaker clouded up and turned gray. There were flashes of light in

the clouded liquid that looked like lightning. There was a muffled explosion. Then the liquid in the beaker cleared and turned an eerie color that glowed green in the dimly lit room.

"Right," said Edgar. "That seems the proper color now."

"It's so beautiful," said Cheyenne.

Edgar poured the contents of the beaker into a glass.

"Here, Mr. Shluffmuffin," he said, "drink this."

Zombie Dad reached out a skeletal hand with rotting fingers.

"On second thought," said Edgar, "I can't risk your dropping it. I'm going to have to feed it to you. Open wide, Mr. Shluffmuffin."

The zombie looked at Edgar blankly.

"Come on, then, Mr. Shluffmuffin," said Edgar. "Open wide. Down the little red lane. Or, in your case, I suppose, down the little *green and black* lane."

"I think Dad's going to need some help," said Wally.

Edgar took a deep breath. Then he tilted Zombie Dad's head back and opened its mouth. The stench that came out of the mouth was so overpoweringly vile that the professor almost fainted, but he managed to pour the contents of the glass down the zombie's throat.

Zombie Dad seemed surprised. He grabbed his neck with both hands and made gurgling, gagging noises. Then he crumpled up and fell backward against the counter. Flasks, beakers, and other laboratory equipment crashed to the floor in an explosion of tinkling shards of glass.

"Dad! What's wrong?" cried Wally.

"Professor, what's happening to him?" cried Cheyenne.

Zombie Dad lay lifeless on the floor. The professor knelt down beside him and felt for a pulse.

"Is he . . . ?" Wally asked.

"Still dead, I'm afraid," said the professor.

The twins stared at their father, who wasn't moving.

"He seems . . . deader than before," said Wally.

"Nonsense," said the professor. "Before I gave him the Elixir of Life, he had no breath, no blood, and no pulse. In short, he was dead. He *still* has no breath, he *still* has no blood, and he *still* has no pulse. How could he be deader now than he was before?"

"Before he was walking around and stuff," said Cheyenne. "And talking. Sort of. Now he's just . . . lying there."

The professor seemed hurt.

"Are you suggesting that my Elixir of Life is a failure?" he asked.

"Well, uh, I wouldn't call it a huge success," said Wally.

"Is that so?" said the professor. He looked even more hurt now. "Firstly, you tell me that before I gave him the elixir, your father was walking. Correction: He was most certainly *not* walking. Staggering, one might say. Stumbling, perhaps. Fumbling. Faltering. Tottering. But most certainly not walking. Secondly, you say he was talking. Correction: He was most certainly *not* talking. Gibbering, one might say. Jabbering. Blithering. Blathering. But most certainly not talking."

"Oh, he was definitely talking," said Cheyenne.

"You think 'Shy, Wa, me Da' is *talking*?" said the professor, his face getting red.

"Yes, I do."

"Then what does it mean?"

"I don't know," said Wally. "Look, if somebody spoke Japanese to you, would you tell me he wasn't talking, just because you didn't know what he was saying?"

"I *would* know what he was saying," said the professor. "I speak Japanese fluently."

"Portuguese, then," said Wally. "What if he was speaking Portuguese?"

"I wrote my doctoral dissertation in Portuguese," said the professor.

Wally threw up his hands. "I give up," he said.

Suddenly, there was a loud noise from the zombie. A noise so loud it made everybody jump. The noise was halfway between a growl

20

and the loudest throat-clearing they had ever heard.

"What was that?" said Cheyenne.

"It came from Dad!" said Wally.

They looked at Zombie Dad. He seemed different. His skin wasn't hanging from his bones quite as much as it had before. It was a little more in place. It looked like it might even be planning to stay there awhile.

Zombie Dad shook his head violently. Then he opened his mouth. Then he stretched his jaws open and shut a few times. Then he made the terrible growling, throat-clearing sound again. Then, in a voice like a rusty gate creaking open, he spoke:

"Hey, gang, what's going on?"

"He can talk!" screamed Cheyenne. "Dad, you can talk!"

"I can?" Dad asked. He looked down at his chest in amazement. "You're right," he said. "That *was* me. Well, I'll be doggoned."

"Dad, you're alive!" shouted Wally. "Professor, he's alive!"

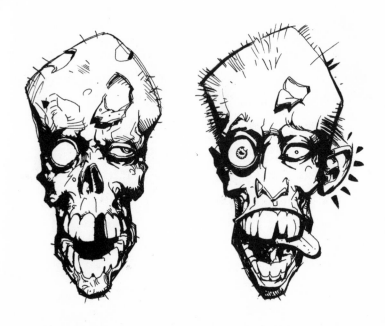

"Oh, is that a fact?" said Edgar coolly, still a little hurt.

The professor knelt down and felt for a pulse. He frowned and shook his head.

"I'm sorry," he said. "I don't seem able to find a pulse."

"But he's alive!" said Cheyenne. "Oh, Daddy, I'm so glad to have you back! I've missed you so much!" She hugged him hard.

"I can't believe we can understand you now,"
said Wally. "It was so awful before, Dad, having
you say stuff and not knowing what you were
talking about." He joined the hug.

The professor was looking all over Dad for a
pulse—in his wrist, in his neck, in his temples,
in his groin, on the inside of his arm—but he
couldn't find one.

"How odd," said the professor. "There's

still no pulse. This has never happened to me before."

There now seemed to be even more skin on Dad's face and body than before. A lot more skin. More hair, even. It had grown back like a Chia Pet in time-lapse photography. And the stench of rotting flesh was getting less disgusting.

"How do you feel, Dad?" asked Cheyenne. She pulled away and looked at him closely.

Dad frowned—he had enough skin on his forehead now to frown. "Gosh, I don't know," he said. "Let me see."

Dad turned his head one way and then the other, raising and lowering his arms and legs, like a farmer checking out rusty farm equipment he'd kept in a barn.

"Everything *seems* to be working okay," Dad reported. "A little stiff, maybe, but otherwise okay. I feel all right, I guess."

"I can't believe it," said Wally. "We have a father again!"

"We're not orphans anymore! That is so unbelievably, incredibly cool!" said Cheyenne. Salty tears welled up in her eyes and spilled down her cheeks.

The professor took out a stethoscope. He put the earpieces in his ears and pressed the opposite end against Dad's chest.

"There is no heartbeat in there at all," said the professor. "I simply do not understand this." He pried open Dad's mouth, cringed at the odor, and peered inside. "My word!" he cried.

"What?" asked Cheyenne.

"Take a look inside here," said Edgar.

Cheyenne looked.

"Eeuuw," said Cheyenne. "His corner teeth are . . ."

". . . inch-long fangs," said the professor. "And take a look at these."

He pointed to something growing now between Dad's shoulder blades—the tops of folded, surprisingly leathery wings. The twins recoiled in shock.

"Dad," said Wally, "there's something gross growing on your back."

"Really?" said Dad. "Boy, am I ever thirsty. I sure could use a drink."

"What can I get you?" asked the professor.

"Oh, I don't know. Anything," said Dad. "A Dr Pepper, or a nice warm glass of human blood would really hit the spot, though."

"Human blood?" said the professor.

"Human blood?" said the twins together.

"Uh, yeah," said Dad. "Why?"

"Hmmm," said the professor, "I'm beginning to understand." He tapped the ashes out of his pipe and filled it with fresh tobacco from a little leather pouch. "The good news, children, is that my Elixir of Life has cured your father's zombiism. The bad news is that it has turned him into a vampire."

"A vampire," Wally repeated. "Wow. So he really *is* still dead."

"Which means we're still orphans," said Cheyenne sadly.

CHAPTER 3

In Case You Think It's Easy, Plotting to Overthrow All Humans on Earth and Use Their Bodily Fluids to Feed Your Larvae—Well, It's Snot

In another part of Dripping Fang Forest, not far from the home of the Spydelles, almost hidden in the dense foliage, stood a Gothic mansion with the outside paint peeling away from its walls like a rattlesnake shedding its skin. Only one lamp burned in the barred windows—the light from an upstairs bedroom.

"Those disgusting orphans!" hissed Dagmar Mandible. "We had them back in our clutches,

Hedy. Then *you* had to go and sink in quicksand and let them slip away."

"Ha! What do you mean *I* let them slip away, dear?" said Hedy Mandible. "*You* were the one who sank in quicksand and let them slip away. *I* was the one who rescued you, remember?"

"It hardly matters who sank in quicksand and who let them slip away," said Dagmar. "The point is, those dreadful children are gone. And now our supply of snot and human foot-stink is so low that the babies are wasting away. If we don't get more soon, the poor things will die of malnutrition."

Dagmar stripped off her four full-length black gloves and tossed them onto the table. With two of her immense black claws she reached upward, grabbed the pink rubbery skin of her face, and peeled it off her head. Dagmar leered at her sister with her gigantic black eyes and her long wavy antennae and her mandibles that looked like a horrid pair of sideways black pliers, only worse.

If Hedy had been human, she would have gasped in horror at the sight. But because she was a giant ant herself, she thought her sister was heartbreakingly beautiful.

CHAPTER 4

Got Blood?

"Would you like a glass of tomato juice, Mr. Shluffmuffin?" Shirley asked.

"Oh sure, thanks," said Dad. "Well, no, on second thought, not really."

They were back in the dining room, sitting around what was left of the table, trying to get used to the miracle that they'd just witnessed. Shirley was once again serving tea and ginger-snaps, glad that Mr. Shluffmuffin wasn't a zombie anymore but not sure how she felt about his being a vampire.

The twins' father was looking lots better now. Nearly all of his skin had grown back, including his nose and ears. So had his hair. His hair was interesting. It was slick and black. It was parted in the center and it formed a *V* in the middle of his forehead.

Wally stared at the *V.* So did Shirley.

"Would you like some V8, Mr. Shluffmuffin?" Shirley asked.

"That's really just tomato juice with some other juices thrown in, right?" Dad asked.

"Well, yes," said Shirley.

"Then, no thanks," said Dad.

"Is there anything else I can offer you?" Shirley asked.

"Oh no, not really," said Dad. "I kind of had my heart set on the human blood thing."

"Have you ever *tasted* human blood, Mr. Shluffmuffin?" asked the professor.

"Well, gosh, no. I just know I'd love it, though."

"Look, Dad, we don't have any human blood here, okay?" said Wally impatiently. "Not unless you plan to start chomping down on one of us when we're not looking, I mean. Uh, you're not going to do that, are you?"

"Of *course* not," said his father, looking away. Wally could tell Dad was offended.

Boy, thought Wally, *first the professor is offended, and now Dad. Everybody is* offended, *for crying out loud. You bring somebody back from the dead and everyone gets all* offended.

"You're just going to have to try drinking something besides human blood, Dad," said Cheyenne.

"Oh, I know that," said Dad crossly. "For pete's sake, don't you think I know that?" He got up and walked out of the room in a huff.

"He's hurt," said Shirley.

"Well, I'm sorry he's hurt," said Wally. "I really am. But if you're a vampire and you're sitting around with your family and friends, having tea and gingersnaps, and you keep asking for a nice warm glass of human blood, you're going to make some people nervous, okay?"

"I guess so," said Cheyenne. "Wally, you don't think Dad would actually try to bite us and suck our blood, do you?"

"How should *I* know what Dad would do?"

said Wally a little too heatedly. "When he was just a dad, he wouldn't. He was a wonderful dad. But then he became a zombie, and then a vampire. I just don't know him anymore, Cheyenne, I really don't. And I certainly don't know what he'd do."

"Well," said Cheyenne, "he may be a vampire now, but he's still my father. And I still love him like crazy. And I still trust him like crazy, too. I do."

"I trust him, too," said Wally. "But I'm still taking a wooden cross and a bag of garlic to bed with me tonight. Shirley, do you happen to have any wooden crosses or bags of garlic I could borrow?"

"In the kitchen, dear. In the cabinet on the left," said Shirley. "Wooden crosses and bags of garlic are in the third drawer. Oh, do you think you'll want a hammer and a wooden stake?"

"In case what, Shirley?" said Wally, his voice rising. "In case I want to drive a stake through my father's heart?"

"*Now* look who's hurt," said Shirley. "Touchy touchy touchy, Wally."

"I'm sorry," said Wally. "It's not easy being a vampire's son."

CHAPTER 5

How Sharper Than a Serpent's Tooth It Is to Have a Child Who's Afraid of a Vampire's Tooth (Assuming You're a Vampire)

That night Shirley found places for everyone to sleep. Cheyenne and Wally had adjoining hammocks in the back bedroom. Dad was given a hammock in the living room. Shirley decided against apologizing that they had no coffins for him to sleep in, fearing that might hurt his feelings.

Dad was slouching on a hammock in the living room, reading. A fire was crackling and popping in the hearth. The twins went in to say good night.

"Good night, Daddy," said Cheyenne. She kissed her father on the cheek, noticing how smooth and cold it felt.

"Good night, Dad," said Wally. He kissed his father on the other cheek, noticing that the zombie stench was gone now, but in its place was another smell. Sort of earthy. Not a bad smell, but perhaps not one you'd want on your

father if you could get something like piney shaving lotion instead.

"Want me to come into your room and sing you a little 'Itsy Bitsy Spider'?" Dad asked.

Wally and Cheyenne exchanged glances.

"Uh, thanks, Dad, not tonight," said Wally. "It's been a pretty busy evening and I'm kind of tired."

"Aww. Too tired to have me sing you to sleep, after not being able to for all these years?" Dad asked.

"Well, uh, yeah," said Wally. "I'm so tired, I'd probably fall asleep right away and miss most of it anyway."

Dad turned toward his daughter.

"What about you, baby? Want your old daddy to sing you a little 'Itsy Bitsy Spider' to put you to sleep?"

"Um, oh, uh, well, actually tonight might not be the best night for that," said Cheyenne. "I mean, I'm pretty tired, too. I do love your singing so much, Daddy, and I really have missed it, but it would be a shame to sleep right through it. Maybe tomorrow night."

"Okay, okay," said Dad. "I know we've been through a lot today, and I can see how it might have tired you out. I'm kind of tired myself. Hey, you're not . . . nervous about being in a dark room with a vampire or anything, are you?" He laughed an uncomfortable little laugh.

"Nervous about . . . ? Oh, Daddy, don't be *silly*," said Cheyenne. "Why would I be nervous about something like *that*? Don't be *ridiculous*."

"That's it, isn't it?" said Dad. "You really *are* scared to be alone with me in the dark." He sighed. "Well, I can't honestly say I blame you. But it still hurts."

"That's not it at all, Daddy," said Cheyenne.

"No, not at all, Dad," said Wally.

"You're sure?"

"Not at all," said Wally. "Okay, well, maybe a little bit. But a *really* little bit."

"How little?" Dad asked.

"Oh, uh, I'd say it's maybe ninety-seven

percent sleepiness and three percent fear of having all the blood sucked out of my body," said Wally. "Not more than three percent, though."

"My numbers would be about the same," said Cheyenne. "Maybe ninety-eight and two."

"That's very sweet," said Dad. "Well, good night, kids. Sleep tight. And don't let the bedbugs bite. Or anything else, for that matter. Ha-ha."

"Ha-ha. Good night, Dad."

"Good night, Dad."

Cheyenne and Wally went into the back bedroom and climbed into their hammocks.

"I feel awful about what we just did," whispered Cheyenne.

"Me, too," whispered Wally.

"Daddy was so hurt that we're afraid of him," whispered Cheyenne. "And I feel terrible about lying to him. By the way, my numbers were actually *two* percent sleepiness and *ninety-eight* percent fear of having all the blood sucked out of my body."

"Me, too," whispered Wally.

"Okay, that's not true, either," whispered

Cheyenne. "It's *zero* percent sleepiness and a *hundred* percent fear of having the blood sucked out of my body."

"Me, too," whispered Wally. "I'm not even sleepy at all. Listen, do you think it would be horrible if I closed our door?"

"It *would* be horrible," whispered Cheyenne. "But do it anyway."

"Right," whispered Wally.

He got quietly out of his hammock and tip-toed to the door, causing the floorboards to creak. He listened a moment, then quietly closed the door.

"And, uh, maybe you could also, you know, uh . . ." whispered Cheyenne.

". . . lock it?" whispered Wally.

"Yeah."

Wally carefully locked the door.

"I *heard* that!" called Dad from the living room.

CHAPTER 6

The Incident in the Bathroom

Humming the theme from Beethoven's Fifth Symphony, Edgar Spydelle lathered up his face with what looked like Reddi-wip. Outside the bathroom window, the sky was just beginning to get light. He sharpened his razor and began to shave.

"Buh buh buh *bumm*, buh buh buh *bumm*...," hummed Edgar.

He hadn't been at it more than a minute when a tiny red bubble of blood appeared in the white shaving lather and began to bloom like a lovely pink flower.

"Oh, drat!" said Edgar under his breath.

He took a wad of toilet paper and wiped the

lather away from the cut. Red liquid welled and dripped.

A shadowy figure materialized in the hall-way outside the bathroom.

"I see you've cut yourself, Professor," said a quiet voice. "May I help you?"

Before Edgar could answer, Sheldon Shluff-muffin was beside him in the tiny bathroom.

"No, no, I'm quite all right, really," said Edgar, who was a little alarmed at Mr. Shluffmuffin's abrupt appearance. "Frightfully decent of you to ask, though."

"Not a problem," said Dad.

"How did you know I cut myself?" asked Edgar.

"Oh, well, I was passing in the hallway and I saw it happen."

"But it's six a.m.," said Edgar. "I didn't think vam—that is, I didn't think people like you would be up and about so early. People like you and Cheyenne and Wally, I mean. People who are *unemployed,* I mean. I mean, you *are* unemployed, are you not?"

43

"I couldn't sleep," said Dad. "Not used to hammocks, I guess. Are you sure I can't help you there, Professor? That looks like a really nasty cut."

"Ah no, thanks, just a nick, got it all under control," said Edgar, chuckling uneasily.

Dad watched in frustration as the little cut on Edgar's neck oozed blood. Finally, unable to control himself, he bent forward and swiftly licked the blood off.

"I'm so sorry, Professor," Dad blurted. "I just couldn't bear to see you bleed all over your shirt."

He hurried out of the bathroom and down the hallway.

"Dad did *what*, Professor?" said Wally. "He licked your *neck*?"

"Quite," said Edgar.

They were in the Spydelles' cheery kitchen. Early-morning sun was warming the room. Birds outside the window were twittering, chirping,

and scolding about tiny birdie matters. Wally was washing the breakfast dishes, and Cheyenne was drying.

"But why would Dad do that?" asked Cheyenne, polishing a plate with a damp cloth.

"I cut myself while shaving," the professor explained.

"We're sorry, Professor," said Cheyenne. "Dad can't help it. He *is* a vampire, you know."

"Yes, I know that," said Edgar. "Despite that—or, actually, because of it—I no longer feel comfortable with your father staying here. Not that I did before, you understand."

Cheyenne and Wally nodded, unable to look at him.

"I'm not saying that he's unwelcome in this house altogether," Edgar continued. "Your father may continue to dine with us, so long as he accepts a totally blood-free diet, of course. He may spend time inside, reading whatever it is that vampires read, as long as we're awake, but not at night when we're asleep."

"Okay," said Wally.

"Okay," said Cheyenne.

"Now, I do appreciate the fact that your father's been dead for several years, and that it's difficult for the dead to find commercial lodging," said Edgar. "So he may spend the nights in our garage if he likes, but not in our house, not anymore. I do hope you understand."

"Okay," said Wally.

"Poor Dad," said Cheyenne. "This is so sad for him. Vampires are people, too."

CHAPTER 7

Infectious Enthusiasm

Thunder rumbled across the lead-colored Cincinnati skies like a gutter ball in the devil's bowling alley. The Mandible sisters made their way along the narrow street to the address they'd gotten off the Internet. The flaked gold lettering on the storefront window read: PATRIOTIC ALL-AMERICAN INSTRUMENT CO. FOUNDED 1945.

Although the shop looked dark, when the sisters tried the door, it squeaked open. They entered. The gloomy store was crammed with musical instruments of every description. From tiny silver piccolos to French horns with snakelike coils of silver tubing, from sassy brass trumpets to gigantic tubas as peppered with pea-sized dents as the surface of the moon.

A gnome with a shaved and polished head materialized out of the gloom. He wore a steel-rimmed monocle jammed in his right eye.

"Ve are clozed," hissed the gnome man in a heavy European accent.

"The door was open," said Dagmar.

"A miztake, zoon to be rectified," said the gnome, locking the door. "But zince you haff managed to slither inzide, vat do you seek?"

"We were looking for something in a nice contagious virus," said Hedy.

The thunder grumbled closer.

"Ve zell muzical inztruments," said the gnome.

"We were told you also sell viruses," said Dagmar.

"You vere mizinformed," said the gnome.

"What a pity," said Dagmar, taking a fat roll of hundred-dollar bills out of her purse. "Now we have nothing to buy with all this money we brought."

The creature considered the roll of bills.

"If ve *did* carry ze viruses," he said, *"vich ve certainly do not,* vat kind vould you haff had in mind?"

"Something that produces sniffling, snuffling, sneezing, coughing, hacking, hocking, spitting, throat-clearing, and serious nose-blowing," said Hedy.

"Something that produces bucketfuls of snot," said Dagmar.

"Znot," repeated the gnome. He nodded.

"Snot is extremely important to us," said Dagmar.

The gnome took out a pack of stinky brown French cigarettes, fitted one into a long platinum cigarette holder, and lit it with a monogrammed platinum cigarette lighter. He sucked on it till the tip of the cigarette glowed bright orange.

"Although ve zell only muzical inztruments," he said, exhaling a cloud of unbelievably putrid smoke in their direction, "zometimes, as a courtezy to our cuztomers, ve carry alzo a few viruses."

"What kind of viruses do you carry, dear?" asked Hedy.

"Ve haff type A influenza, which is ze most videspread variety. Nearly zixty percent of flu viruses are type A, und it iss ze cause of most major vorldvide epidemics of influenza. Type B iss less common und less severe. Type C iss rather uncommon, und it causes only mild disease."

"Oh, pooh on B and C," said Hedy. "Tell me, dear, which do you recommend, the viruses or the bacteria?"

"Ze bacterial infections can be quite severe, und zey can even lead to death," said the gnome with an evil leer. "Unfortunately, zey can usually be viped out like *zat*—poof!—by ze antibiotics. Ze beauty of ze viral infections iss zat ze anti-biotics cannot touch zem."

"I do like the sound of *that*," said Hedy.

"As a courtezy to our customers," the gnome continued, releasing another cloud of putrid cigarette smoke in the Mandible sisters' direction, "ve haff chust received a rare shipment of ze famous Spanish influenza virus of 1918. Zat was a *very* goot year for ze influenza. Vould you be interested in zomezing like zat?"

"Absolutely," said Dagmar.

"Und tell me, vould zis be for your own perzonal use, or do you intend to . . . share it vit others?"

"Share it with others," said Dagmar. "*Lots* of others."

"Goot. In zat case, ve vould recommend ze atomizer dispensers," said the gnome. "Vould you be interested in zum of dose?"

"Oh, most definitely, dear," said Hedy. "Most definitely."

CHAPTER 8

He Knows When You Are Sleeping

Moonlight poured into the Spydelles' garage through a skylight, whitewashing the figure in the overhead rafters. Banished to the garage, hanging upside down like a bat, Dad Shluffmuffin sulked.

To be a zombie or to be a vampire, he mused, *that is the question. Whether 'tis nobler in the mind to nibble human flesh or to slurp up human blood. 'Tis a sorry choice at best, because either way you're dead.*

Unfolding leathery wings like sections of an umbrella, Dad let go of the overhead beam and glided noiselessly to the ground.

Neither way do you escape the pain of children

who fear to have you sing about itsy bitsy spiders to them in the dark but who do not fear sleeping in a house with an enormous, hairy eight-legged real *spider. Talk about* irony, *man—sheesh!*

Dad took out a pocket comb and slicked back the black hair on both sides of his head. Then he walked to the door of the garage, opened it, and slipped outside.

The night smells intrigued him. The fragrant earth, the heady aroma of pine needles, the slightly sweet smell of rotting vegetation. As a human he had hardly noticed night smells. As a zombie he had had no awareness of them, at least not since his nose had dropped off and fallen into the swamps.

Dad glided quietly up to the door of the Spydelle house. He tried the knob and found the door locked. He smiled. Locks were meant to keep out humans and wolves, but vampires knew certain useful tricks.

Dad knelt down in front of the door, his knees pressing into the hard stone of the doorstep. He stuck out a long, pointed, red vampire tongue and licked the doorknob. It tasted brassy. Inside the lock he heard tumblers tumble. He stood up and tried the knob again. The door creaked slowly inward.

Dad crept inside and drew the door shut behind him.

Once inside the house, he listened for the sounds of those who slept vulnerably within, innocent of his entrance. What would be their reaction now if they awoke and sensed his presence? Shrieks? Screams? Tearing of hair? Gnashing of teeth? Probably.

Why had he entered the house? He himself wasn't sure. He crept quietly across the entryway, past the living room where once he'd been trusted to sleep, and then paused outside the

door to his children's bedroom. He tried the knob, and found it locked against him.

Chuckling without mirth, he licked the knob and heard the tumblers click. He entered the darkened bedroom.

He heard the soft breathing of the children he loved, able to tell them apart through sound alone. Cheyenne's breathing was snuffly, her nasal passages clogged with phlegm. Wally's breathing was clear and shallow, but the stench of his bare feet was nearly enough to knock his father to the floor.

Dad approached his sleeping son and daughter. He gazed down at them in their adjoining hammocks and sighed. How he adored them. How he ached for the three of them to be a family again. And how they had hurt him. Through his vampire's eyes he could see them in a green phosphorescent X-ray glow, could see the tiny veins in their cheeks and temples as though their skin were cellophane, could see the purple blood as it pulsed rhythmically through the small carotid arteries in their necks.

Blood! No, no, he dared not think about blood, not now! His craving for blood was over-powering. He craved blood the way a man crossing the Mojave Desert and dying of thirst craves a frosty glass of ice-cold lemonade with a clear flexible straw, a sprig of mint, and a jaunty little paper parasol.

But he couldn't take his eyes off Cheyenne's carotid artery, beating now like a tiny timepiece, like the heart of a baby bird, the blood pulsing like Welch's purple grape juice through a clear flexible straw with a sprig of mint and a jaunty little . . .

Unable to control himself, Dad suddenly bent down, his vampire fangs an inch from his sleeping daughter's throat.

A single bite now on each of my precious children's necks would be so easy, he mused. *It would make them immortal! It would bind them to me forever! And what would be the harm in giving my babies eternal life? Together the three of us could watch human history unspool, could watch the centuries peel away like onion layers, could watch Cincinnati*

prosper and grow into a mighty city-state, could watch
mankind be gradually replaced by robots and the sun
slowly cool to a glowing ember in the grate of the ce-
lestial hearth. Plus which, the taste of human blood
right about now would really hit the spot—oh man,
would it ever.

NO!

Revolted at what he'd nearly talked himself
into doing, Dad merely pressed his lips to Cheyenne's neck in a fatherly kiss. Then he tousled
the hair of his sleeping son and tiptoed out of
the bedroom, closed the door behind him, and
licked it locked.

Cheyenne moaned and stirred in her hammock.
In her dream her father was no longer a vampire
or a zombie but the Dad she used to know and
love, taking her and Wally to the circus, buying
them pink lemonade and cotton candy, even
though cotton candy was always such a disap-
pointment, looking so pink and fluffy and full of
promise but tasting more like cotton than candy

and always chewing down to a depressing little clump of sugary nothing.

She longed for the old days when Dad had had a pulse, didn't lose body parts or thirst for blood. She hated to think those days were gone forever.

In Wally's dream his father played catch with him in a golden field of wheat. The ball and his arm and his father's arm and everything else in the scene were moving in slow motion.

"Dad, why is everything moving in slow motion?" Wally called.

"Because this is a *dream,* son," Dad called back cheerily. "Everything in dreams always moves in slow motion. At least it does in movies."

Vampire Dad crept into Edgar and Shirley's bedroom. An enormous hammocklike web stretched the full length of the room. In the middle of the web lay Shirley in her silk pajamas, looking smaller now in sleep, six of her eight legs tucked beneath her, cradling her relatively tiny husband with her two forelegs like a treasured teddy bear.

Edgar's throat looked fairly tasty, but Dad didn't relish leaning over Shirley's eight hairy spider legs to get to it.

Dad crept quietly into Edgar's closet. He surveyed the line of starched white lab coats and took one off a hanger. From the top of the dresser he took a stethoscope and a rectangular blue plastic name tag that read: *Dr. Edgar Spydelle.* He crept out of the bedroom and across the living room and out of the house.

In the driveway was the Spydelles' van. Dad climbed in, realized he had no car keys, so instead bent down and breathed electrical energy into the ignition. The engine hiccupped and sputtered and started with a cough. Then, without bothering to turn on the headlights, Dad drove down the driveway and along the narrow path and out of Dripping Fang Forest to the highway.

By the time he had pulled up at the emergency room entrance of Cincinnati General, it was nearly 4:00 a.m. He parked, put on Edgar's white lab coat, and draped the stethoscope around his neck the way he'd seen doctors do on TV. He climbed out of the van and walked confidently into the too-bright ER.

The hospital was very quiet. There were no patients on either beds or gurneys. Behind the counter a nurse and a lab technician were playing video games.

"Excuse me," said Dad. "I'm Dr. Spydelle. I'm going to need thirty to forty units of whole blood right away. Can you tell me where to find that?"

"What do you need with so much blood, Doctor?" asked the nurse.

"For, um, some operations I plan to be doing pretty soon," said Dad.

"But, Doctor, there aren't any patients here," said the nurse.

"Oh, well, no, of *course* there aren't any patients here," said Dad. "Not *yet*, I mean. But there will be very shortly, don't you worry about *that*. There was an accident out on the highway, a terrible fourteen-car accident. Yeah. Mangled bodies all over the place. Yards of glistening intestines. A regular smorgasbord of blood and guts. I'm expecting patients to be arriving here by the busload any minute now."

"We didn't get any calls about a terrible accident or about any patients on the way here," said the nurse.

"Well, of course not. That's because they're trying to keep it quiet," said Dad. "They don't want to start a panic. If you'll just point the way to the blood room, I'll start getting ready. Washing my hands and stuff. *Scrubbing up,* I believe we doctors call it."

The nurse pointed.

"It's right through there," she said.

In a large stainless-steel refrigerator marked CAUTION! HUMAN BLOOD!, Dad found what he was looking for—stacks of thick plastic bags filled with purplish fluid. Each one had a little plastic tube at the top with a cap at the end. Dad was so giddy with pleasure, his knees grew weak.

He grabbed as many bags as he could carry,

but the nearness of all that purple deliciousness was just too tempting.

Maybe just a taste, he thought. *Maybe just a drop. Maybe just enough to wet my lips.*

He put all the bags of blood down on a table, opened one, and placed the tube between his lips.

The first drop was like a mouthful of mushy cream-filled Hostess Twinkies to a starving man. It landed on his tongue and radiated pleasure outward in waves throughout his entire body. He sucked hard on the tube. He sucked so hard that blood dribbled down his chin onto his starched white lab coat.

The nurse walked into the room, saw what Dad was doing, and stopped short.

"This isn't what it looks like," said Dad. "I assure you, I can explain. I was just—"

The nurse's screams drowned out his explanation.

Still clutching the half-empty blood bag, Dad fled from the room, raced through the clinic, and burst out of the emergency entrance before the sleeping security guard could be awakened.

He leaped into the Spydelles' van, yanked the door shut, and breathed life into the ignition. He stomped on the accelerator and tore out of the parking lot so fast he left black rubber streaks on the pavement. Swerving to avoid the lampposts, fireplugs, and parked cars that kept darting into his path, Dad drove back to the Spydelles', parked the van, slipped into the garage, and returned to his perch up in the rafters before the sky got pink.

CHAPTER 9

The Phone Call That Changed Everything

Shirley was the kind of spider who for a ringing phone dropped exactly nothing. During the first twelve rings, she washed up the morning dishes. During the next twelve, she repaired a

hole in her bedroom web. On the twenty-fifth ring, she picked up the receiver and spoke.

"This is Shirley," she said.

"Mrs. Spydelle?" said an unfamiliar voice. "This is Hortense Jolly, owner and founder of the Jolly Days Orphanage of Greater Cincinnati. May I speak freely?"

"Sure," said Shirley.

"Not long ago, Mrs. Spydelle, you and your husband came to Jolly Days to look over our latest crop of orphans. I was surprised that you preferred to remain outside in the van, but your husband explained that you were a bit self-conscious about your, uh . . . about the fact that you . . ."

"That I'm an enormous spider with eight hairy legs?" said Shirley. "You don't need to mince words with me. I happen to be quite comfortable with who I am, Miss Jolly. I was just being sensitive to the feelings of others, yours and the orphans'."

"Well, you needn't worry about *my* feelings, Mrs. Spydelle. I do business with all sorts of

68

people, no matter *how* revolting they may look. To tell the truth, I never even *notice* how they look. And you may be interested to know that I've placed *dozens* of my orphans with giant insects. In fact, just the other day I placed two of my orphans with a pair of disgusting giant—"

"I'm not an *insect,* Miss Jolly," said Shirley. "I'm an *arachnid.*"

"Of course, dear, of course. The reason I phoned, though, is that when your husband was here, he seemed very interested in adopting one or more of our lovely orphans. They were quite taken with him, too, I might add. He promised to get back to us by the end of the day, but, sadly, he never called. I can't imagine why. Can you tell me why he never called?"

"Well, to be frank, Miss Jolly, the children he described seemed to have so many problems. There was the little boy who wets the bed and weighs over two hundred pounds..."

"Rocco," said Hortense. "He no longer wets the bed. And he may eat a lot, but as I pointed out to your husband, he'll eat things you were going to throw out anyway, stuff that's gone bad in the fridge. He's so handy to have around."

"Yes," said Shirley. "Then there was the little boy whose teeth are too soft to eat anything but pudding or wet bread . . ."

"Orville," said Hortense. "What an angel. He doesn't mind taking out the garbage, and he finds such interesting things in it, things that he makes into charming jewelry for fun and profit."

"Right," said Shirley. "Then there was the little girl who speaks only Polish and another one who is covered with sores . . ."

"Rosie and Ellie May," said Hortense. "Rosie knows seven words in English now—isn't that scrumptious? And as I told your husband, the doctor says most of Ellie May's sores will probably heal. She can also run very fast, if it's downhill and you give her a little push."

"Then there was the boy who sets fires and steals," said Shirley. "In fact, he stole my husband's watch during his visit."

"That would be Wayne," said Hortense. "As I

told your husband, Wayne has definitely *stopped* setting fires. And if he steals something, he always gives it right back. Did your husband mention that Wayne gave the watch *right back*?"

"It doesn't matter," said Shirley. "The point is, we just didn't feel, after talking it over, that any of the children he described were ... quite right for us."

"The orphans were *so* disappointed, poor darlings," said Hortense. "Oh, they're used to rejection by now, of course. They have to be. They have to deal with it so often, unfortunately. If they cry, it's always off in the corner where I can't see their tears."

When she heard this, something inside Shirley collapsed.

"The children cry because we aren't adopting them?" she asked in a whisper.

"Poor sweet little things," said Hortense, sensing a sudden advantage. "I wish I could give them all lots of hugs, but there are so many of them. If I tried, my arms would get all stretched out of shape. Ha-ha. Would you like to come out here and hug a few orphans, Mrs. Spydelle? With all those arms of yours, I'll bet you could hug quite a few of them at once."

"I can't bear the crying of little children," said Shirley, beginning to sob.

"Then perhaps you'd like to adopt a few of the poor wretches," said Hortense. "Our usual fee is six hundred per orphan, but we do offer group rates. You could have three for seven-fifty, four for eight-fifty, five for nine hundred even. Just tell me how many you can use, and I'll work with you, Mrs. Spydelle—oh, may I call you Spidey?"

"I'm afraid I . . . can't speak now . . . ," said Shirley through her sobs.

She hung up the receiver, went into the bedroom, and threw herself on her web.

I cannot stand life without children any longer! she thought.

CHAPTER 10

The Worst Choice You Will Ever Have to Make

When Edgar Spydelle came in from work that night, everybody was lounging in the family room. Shirley was spinning silk to make pajamas for the twins. Cheyenne was writing in her diary. Wally was thumbing through the Spydelles' set of encyclopedias. Dad was reading up on vampires.

"Evening, all," said Edgar, filling his pipe with fragrant tobacco.

"I had a phone call today from Hortense Jolly at the orphanage," said Shirley.

"Uh-oh," said Wally. "She's not trying to get us back, is she?"

"I sure hope not," said Cheyenne. "Not that

73

living at the orphanage was so terrible, but I really love it so much more here with *you* guys."

"No," said Shirley, "she didn't even mention you two. She was calling to make me feel guilty about not adopting those orphans you looked at, Edgar."

"Oh my," said Edgar, holding a match to the bowl of his pipe.

"She's great at making people feel guilty," said Wally.

"I do hope you're not having second thoughts about those orphans," said Edgar. "They were quite a ghastly lot."

"All I know is," said Shirley, "when she told me how disappointed they were at not being adopted by us, how they were crying quietly in the corner, my heart went out to them, Edgar. Maybe we should reconsider. Do you think we should?"

"I don't want to say bad things about the kids I used to live with," said Wally, "but you might not be too happy with them."

"Well, that phone call made me realize how

desperately I need to start a family," said Shirley. "If we don't adopt some orphans soon, then I'm really going to have to insist on having babies with *you*, Edgar."

Edgar exhaled so suddenly he blew burning embers out of the bowl of his pipe.

"My word, Shirley!" he exclaimed. "Surely you're not serious!"

"Quite serious, Edgar."

"B-but you realize that afterward you'd have to eat me, don't you?"

Shirley began to sniff and dab at her eyes.

"It's not something I *want* to do, Edgar," she said. "I'd miss you terribly, of course. I *would*. You're my husband. I *love* you, dearest. But my need to have a family is . . . very strong."

There was silence as everybody in the room thought about what Shirley had just said. Wally and Cheyenne exchanged long questioning looks. Then they nodded to each other.

"Shirley," said Wally, "what about adopting *us*?"

Now it was Dad's turn to be surprised.

"*Adopting* you?" said Dad. "Wally, what are you saying? *They* can't adopt you. *Nobody* can adopt you. *I* happen to be your father, young man."

"I know you are, Dad," said Wally gently, "but you can't really take care of us anymore, can you? I mean, you're dead. Also, you're a vampire."

"Well, maybe I *am*," said Dad. "So what? Is that my fault?"

"No, Dad, of course it's not your fault," said Cheyenne.

"Well, I absolutely refuse to allow you to be adopted by anybody else," said Dad. "You kids are my own flesh and blood. The idea of letting you be adopted by somebody else makes me crazy enough to . . . to bite!"

Edgar and Shirley both shrank back in alarm.

"Now, now, Dad, don't get excited," said Wally.

"He doesn't mean that literally," Cheyenne explained to the frightened Spydelles.

"How do you know that?" asked Edgar.

"The only way I'd let the Spydelles adopt you," said Dad, "is if you can look me straight in the eye and tell me you love them more than you love me. Can you do that, Wally? Can you do that, Cheyenne? Well, can you?"

Neither Cheyenne nor Wally could look at him at all.

When the twins walked into Edgar's lab that night, the professor was mixing green and purple chemicals in a glass beaker.

"We've talked it over, Professor, and we've come to a decision," said Wally.

"We've decided to tell Dad we love you and Shirley more than him," said Cheyenne. She was sniffing and snuffling and blowing her nose harder than ever.

"I appreciate what you children are trying to do," said Edgar, "but I cannot allow you to do it."

"You don't have a choice, sir," said Cheyenne. "Unless you adopt us, Shirley will insist on having children of her own, and that means she'll have to eat you."

"I've thought this over at great length," said Edgar. "I am willing to sacrifice my own life so that you can be with your real father. It is a far, far better thing I do now than I have ever done."

"Well, thanks, but we refuse to let you give your life for us," said Wally. "We're going out to the garage now to tell Dad."

"It will be painful for him," said Cheyenne, "but he'll get over it."

"As bad as it will be for Dad," said Wally, "it

will be much worse for you if Shirley has to eat you."

"I forbid you to do this," said Edgar weakly.

"Sir, I'm afraid you don't have anything to say about this," said Cheyenne.

Wally and Cheyenne walked out of the house. The night was alive with bug sounds. Crickets cricking, katydids katying, ratchet bugs ratcheting. Far in the distance, they could hear the howling of wolves.

They walked toward the garage, then stopped.

"We don't have to do this," said Cheyenne.

"We *can't* do this," said Wally.

"We *must* do this," said Cheyenne. She broke into sobs and sneezes, then stopped abruptly. "Poor Dad," she whispered.

"All right," said Wally. "Let's get this over with."

They knocked on the garage door. A moment later, Dad opened it.

"Well, hi, kids," said Dad. "Come to kiss me good night?"

"Uh, not exactly," said Cheyenne.

"Dad, we have something to tell you," said Wally.

"Something painful," said Cheyenne.

"What is it?" Dad asked, his voice suddenly made of wood.

"Dad, we, uh . . . we love the Spydelles more than we love you," Wally blurted, choking off a sob.

Dad tried not to show any emotion. He looked out the garage window. Even though it was completely dark, with his vampire vision he could see the point where the dense forest had been cut back to permit the Spydelles' house to be built. It seemed that the tree line had grown closer to the house since the last time he'd looked. Was that possible, that the trees could actually be moving closer to the house?

"It's because I'm dead and I drink human blood, isn't it," said Dad finally, not looking at either of his children, a statement more than a question.

"It's not just that, Dad," said Wally. "It's a *lot* of things."

"It's not *you*, Dad, it's *us*," added Cheyenne. "We just need to have two parents, like we used to when Mom was alive, that's all."

When Mom was alive . . . , Dad thought. What a happy family they had been when Sharon Shluffmuffin was alive, before she'd been so savagely attacked by that gang of vicious bunnies at the petting zoo. Before he, Sheldon Shluffmuffin, had fallen through the seat of the Porta Potti at the Cincinnati circus and drowned. Before tiny forty-nine-pound Grandma Gloria Shluffmuffin had fallen asleep in her backyard wearing a black sleep mask and been carried off by a nearsighted eagle that mistook her for a raccoon. How things had changed since then! If only they could return to those golden pre–Porta Potti, pre–vicious-bunny, pre–nearsighted-eagle days . . .

"So you're telling me you'd rather have a . . . a disgusting giant *spider* for a parent than a vampire?" Dad asked quietly, squeezing all emotion out of his voice.

"Yes," said Wally.

"Yes," said Cheyenne.

Dad squinted out the window. He could have sworn he'd actually caught the trees moving toward the house just then. Maybe only a millimeter, but still.

"All right, fine. Let them adopt you," said Dad. He laughed bitterly. "To have his own children prefer to live with a giant spider—*that* is truly The Vampire's Curse! If you don't mind now, children, I'd like to be alone."

They shuffled out of the garage. Dad slammed the door hard behind them.

CHAPTER 11

Let's Get the Feds onto the Onts

Cheyenne stirred in her sleep. There was something . . . wrong. Something terrible very close by. Something . . . evil.

Wally stirred, and awoke. He, too, had sensed something dangerous very close at hand. He opened his eyes. He glanced at the shade pulled down over their bedroom window.

Shadows danced on the shade. Trees from the forest, blowing in the wind of the predawn night. Somewhere in the distance wolves howled and a small creature cried out in pain. It was the hour of the wolf. The time when the worst things of the night tend to happen.

There was something wrong about the shadows on that shade. About the way they were moving. They no longer looked like shadows from trees.

Wally looked over at Cheyenne. She was sitting up in bed, staring at the shadows on the shade.

Wally put his finger to his lips and wriggled quietly out of his hammock.

He moved softly toward the window. Ten feet away. Now eight. Now five. Now three. He reached out and gripped the bottom of the window shade. He tugged it down smartly, then let it go. The shade shot upward, flapping noisily.

There in the window, staring in at them, were two ghastly faces. The Mandible sisters!

Cheyenne screamed.

Dagmar tugged at the window, forcing it up a couple of inches, then thrust gloved hands through the opening, gripping the bottom of the window and trying to lift it higher.

Wally flung himself at the window and

shoved it downward with all his might. Dagmar shrieked a piercing unearthly, insectlike cry, yanked backward, and fled.

A long black glove remained on the windowsill. It was probably just an illusion in the moonlight, but Wally thought he saw the glove twitch.

"Are you sure it was them?" asked Shirley.

She was standing at the stove in her blue silk dressing gown, making breakfast for the twins. French toast with green jelly. She assured them it was pine jelly, not anything spider-produced that might make them want to puke.

"It was them all right," said Wally, holding up the glove.

"There aren't too many faces that look like Dagmar and Hedy," said Cheyenne.

"I think they're planning to make their move on us soon," said Wally.

"We've got to do something," said Cheyenne. "Not only to save ourselves but to save mankind. They *are* planning to replace mankind with a race of super-ants."

"But we can't stop them ourselves," said Wally. "We're afraid of them."

"Why don't you go to the police?" asked Shirley.

"We can't," said Wally. "If we do, they'll take us back to the Onts. Just like they tried to do last time."

"Maybe if we really explain it well this time, the police will believe us and help us," said Cheyenne.

"Yeah, right, like *that's* going to happen," said Wally.

"Then what about the FBI?" said Shirley. "Don't they have something to do with stopping people from taking over mankind and ending life on Earth as we know it?"

"You know, that's a great idea, Shirley," said Cheyenne. "Let's go to the FBI, Wally."

"If you like, Edgar can drop you off there on his way to the museum," said Shirley.

———

"May I help you?" asked the FBI receptionist. She wore a slim black headset, black-rimmed glasses, and a frown. The great seal of the Federal Bureau of Investigation took up much of the space on the wall behind her head. On her desk were a phone and a clipboard.

"Yes," said Wally. "We need to talk to somebody about a problem."

"What sort of problem would this be?" asked the receptionist.

"A problem of someone plotting to take over Earth," said Cheyenne.

"I see," said the receptionist. She consulted the clipboard on her desk. "And would the plotting parties be Communist Spies, Muslim Terrorists, Liberal Democrats, Aliens from Outer Space, or Other?"

"Uh, I guess Other," said Cheyenne.

The receptionist made a checkmark on her clipboard.

"I see, and may I ask the nature of your Other?"

"Giant ants," said Wally.

"I see," said the receptionist. "Now, when we say giant ants, would we be speaking of individuals half an inch in length or larger?"

"Larger. Much larger."

"Very well," said the receptionist. "In these cases the Bureau recommends you try ant traps and, failing that, a good exterminator. You can look in the Yellow Pages under *Exterminators.*"

"These ants are over six feet tall and have season tickets to all Cincinnati Reds home games," said Wally.

"I see," said the receptionist. "So these would not be your usual type of giant ants."

"No, they wouldn't," said Wally.

"Then perhaps you should speak to one of our agents."

"Yes, thank you," said Wally. "That would be a good idea."

"One moment please."

The receptionist buzzed somebody on her intercom.

"Sir," she said, "there are two children here

who wish assistance with ants that have season tickets to Cincinnati Reds home games. Yes, sir, I did suggest the ant traps and the exterminator. Well, it seems these ants are plotting to take over Earth. I don't know, sir."

She turned to the children. "By what means are they planning to take over Earth?" she asked.

"By breeding hundreds of super-larvae in their basement and enslaving the human race," said Wally.

"By breeding hundreds of super-larvae in their basement and enslaving the human race, sir," said the receptionist. "Yes, sir. I'll send them right in."

The receptionist wrote their names on temporary passes and stuck one on each of their chests.

"Down that hall there to room 2059," she said.

"Thanks," said Cheyenne.

Cheyenne and Wally walked down a very long hallway. They passed many musty-smelling offices filled with floor-to-ceiling file cabinets. They arrived at room 2059 and went in.

A man with white hair and a nice suntan sat behind a desk, eating pistachio nuts from a blue ceramic bowl. The man had a frowning smile on his face. The pistachios themselves seemed to be smiling—a bowl of tiny smiling parrot-nuts with partly opened beaks, enjoying a secret joke.

"Hello there," said the man. "I'm Special Agent Tom Cromwell."

"I'm Wally Shluffmuffin, and this is my sister, Cheyenne," said Wally.

"You the kids with the ant problem?"

"Yes, sir," said Wally. "They are two giant ants, they live in Dripping Fang Forest, and their names are Dagmar and Hedy Mandible. They're sisters."

Cromwell never stopped picking smiling pistachios out of their shells and popping them into his mouth. Grains of salt ringed his lips like stubble missed in shaving.

"The gal at the desk says you think these ants are going to enslave the human race. That right?"

"Yes, sir," said Wally.

"And what makes you think that, son?"

"Because they said, 'We're going to enslave the human race,'" said Wally.

Cromwell chuckled. "I gotta hand it to you guys," he said. "That is one funny put-on you got there."

"This isn't a put-on," said Wally. "You think this is a put-on?"

"Yep, and a good one," said Cromwell. "Believe me when I tell you that I've had all kinds of put-ons tried on me, but this is one of the most original."

"Okay," said Wally, "what if a grown-up, a grown-up you respect, told you this was not a put-on, sir? Would you believe *him*?"

"You have somebody like that you want me to talk to, son?"

"Yes. How about Professor Edgar Spydelle, head of the Bug Department at the Cincinnati Museum of Natural History and Science? Have you ever heard of him?"

"Spydelle? Yeah, sure, I've heard of Spydelle. Who hasn't? He's a famous guy. You actually know him?"

"Yes," said Wally. "Would you call him?"

"Why not?"

Cromwell took out a Cincinnati directory, looked up the number, and dialed.

"Professor Spydelle, please," said Cromwell into the phone. "Special Agent Cromwell, Federal Bureau of Investigation. Thank you. Hello, Professor Spydelle? This is Special Agent Cromwell, Federal Bureau of Investigation. Right. Professor, I'm sitting here with two kids who claim to know you, Wally and . . . ?"

Cromwell looked at Cheyenne with a questioning expression.

". . . Cheyenne Shluffmuffin," said Cheyenne.

"Wally and Cheyenne Shlerfmurfin," said Cromwell. "They've just told me a marvelous story about giant ants, which they *swear* is on the up-and-up, but I . . . Yeah? Really? You don't say. Well, that's very interesting, Professor. Yeah.

You don't say. Well, thank you, Professor, I appreciate your help."

Cromwell hung up the phone. He was no longer smiling.

"Spydelle says you kids are telling the truth," said Cromwell. "I thought you were putting me on."

"So what are you going to do now?" asked Cheyenne. "Are you going to send in a SWAT team to arrest the Mandibles?"

"No, no, not yet," said Cromwell. "You don't just send in a SWAT team without scoping out the situation. First, I'm going to send in one of my finest undercover investigators to scope out the situation. If he tells me it's a go, *then* I send in the SWAT team."

"How soon are you sending this undercover investigator?" asked Wally.

"Right now," said Cromwell. "Right this minute."

"Can we wait here for him to come back and hear what he says?" asked Cheyenne.

"It might take a while," said Cromwell.

"We've got lots of time," said Cheyenne. "Can we wait for him to come back?"

"I guess so, but not in my office," said Cromwell. "You'll have to wait for him out there in the waiting area."

CHAPTER 12

Master of the Subtle Art of Undercover Investigation

The gray Chevy Caprice with the big official gold seal of the U.S. Census Bureau on both front doors sped out of Cincinnati and made its way along the highway.

As Special Agent Steve McCobb drove, the buildings of the city were replaced by empty lots filled with old tires and rusting truck parts. Then the empty lots filled with old tires and rusting truck parts were replaced by dense forest. The gray Chevy Caprice slowed at a break in the trees and stopped.

Over the arched opening into the woods was a sign: DRIPPING FANG FOREST. Next to this sign was a smaller sign: PRIVATE PROPERTY. KEEP OUT. THIS MEANS YOU. TRESPASSERS WILL BE . . .

The word PROSECUTED had been crossed out and somebody had written SHOT above it. The word SHOT had been crossed out, and somebody had written TORN APART BY WOLVES above that.

Special Agent Steve McCobb squinted at the sign and chuckled. He chuckled because when he first read it, he figured it was a joke, but then he stopped in mid-chuckle. There was something eerie about the sign. To reassure himself, McCobb patted the bulge beneath his sport coat. A .38 caliber Smith & Wesson in a shoulder holster. It made him feel a little better. He drove under the sign and entered the forest.

The road that went into the forest wasn't blacktopped like the highway, wasn't even gravel-topped. It seemed to be just matted-down grass and vines. After about fifty yards, the dense vegetation on all sides of the narrow road forced McCobb to abandon the car, remove his attaché case, and proceed on foot. In another thirty yards, he came across what looked like a car completely choked by vines.

Upon close inspection, McCobb discovered the lettering on the car door read: CINCINNATI METRO POLICE. There was nobody inside the car. He wondered nervously why the two cops assigned to the patrol car had abandoned it. McCobb walked on.

After walking for another twenty minutes, catching brief glimpses of possibly empty houses through the trees, McCobb reached a brown Gothic mansion that looked badly in need of repair. Old paint peeled away from the house in strips, like the exoskeleton of a molting scorpion. The number on the door of the building matched the one Cromwell had gotten from the Shluffmuffin kids, so he rang the doorbell. He heard the sound reverberate deep within.

For a moment he thought no one was at home, but then the door opened. A tall lady in a wide-brimmed black hat and large black sunglasses stood in the doorway. He wondered why she'd been wearing sunglasses inside the house.

"Hello, ma'am," he said. "My name is McCobb. I'm from the U.S. Census Bureau. I wonder if I might take a moment of your time and ask you a couple of questions?"

"I'm in kind of a hurry," said the lady in the sunglasses. "Will this take long?"

"No, ma'am, not long at all. May I come inside?"

"Of course, dear," she said. She motioned him inside.

Well, so far so good, he thought. *She seems harmless enough. She even called me* dear. *I wonder when I get to meet the giant ants.*

He walked into the house and was immediately struck by how much cleaner it looked on the inside than it had on the outside. The floor in the hallway was so clean and so highly polished he could have used it for a bowling alley. He noticed an odd coppery smell. From somewhere came a curious sound: *Ch-ch-ch-ch-ch . . . Ch-ch-ch-ch-ch . . .*

"Well now," said the lady, ushering him into what looked like the dining room. "Why don't we sit down right here and you can ask me whatever you'd like."

They sat down at the table. He opened his attaché case and took out his clipboard.

"Okay," he said, pencil poised above the paper. "What is your name?"

"Mandible," said the lady. "Hedy Mandible. Would you like some cookies and milk, dear?"

"No thanks, ma'am. How many people are living at this address?"

"Just two. Me and my sister, Dagmar."

"Are you employed?"

"We are self-employed, dear."

"What is the nature of your business?"

"We're breeders. Breeders of small animals."

"Are you breeding super-ant larvae to enslave humans and end life on Earth as we know it?"

"My heavens, no," said Hedy, laughing good-naturedly.

McCobb laughed, too.

"You're not going to believe this," he said, "but we actually got some crackpot report that you and your sister are giant ants and you are breeding super-ant larvae to enslave humans and end life on Earth as we know it."

Hedy shrieked with laughter. "Dagmar!" she called. "You've got to come here and listen to this!"

Another lady in a wide-brimmed black hat entered the dining room. She was even taller than Hedy. She, too, wore sunglasses. *Why are they wearing sunglasses inside the house?* McCobb wondered again.

"Dagmar, this is Mr. McCobb from the Census Bureau. Mr. McCobb, this is my sister, Dagmar. Tell her what you just told me, dear."

"I was just telling your sister that we actually got some crackpot report that you two are giant ants and you are breeding super-ant larvae to enslave humans and end life on Earth as we know it."

Dagmar and Hedy burst into raucous laughter.

"Giant *ants*!" screamed Hedy. "I love it! I just *love* it! Who did you say gave you this report?"

"A couple of kids," said McCobb.

"Do you happen to recall their names?" asked Dagmar. "We have a mischievous niece and nephew who are always playing pranks on us. Was it Walter and Cheyenne Shluffmuffin?"

"I think those are the names all right," said McCobb. "Shluffmuffin."

"Why would our niece and nephew be giving reports to the U.S. Census Bureau?" asked Dagmar.

"Oh, shucks, I'm not really from the Census Bureau," said McCobb with a smile. He took out his badge. "I'm Special Agent McCobb. Federal Bureau of Investigation. You know, I might as well phone in my report."

He took out his cell phone and dialed a number.

"Chief, it's McCobb," he said into the phone. "I'm at the Mandible house now. Talking to two lovely ladies named Hedy and Dagmar Mandible. Nothing suspicious here. There seems to be no truth to the allegation that the Mandibles are giant ants breeding super-ant larvae to enslave humans and end life on Earth as we know it." He chuckled. "Right, Chief. Yeah, you might as well send those kids home now."

McCobb flipped his cell phone closed and put his clipboard back in his attaché case. "Well, sorry to have bothered you ladies," he said, standing up.

"Not at all," said Hedy. "It was worth it, just for the laughs."

They led him toward the front door. On the way they passed the entrance to the cellar. Above it was a sign: CELLAR. DO NOT ENTER.

"What's down there?" asked McCobb.

"Just the cellar," said Hedy.

"I might as well have a look," said McCobb.

"Really?" said Dagmar.

"Yeah, as long as I'm here," said McCobb. "When I get back, my chief is going to ask me if I saw it." He winked. "The census taker must investigate to discover any aliens who might be living in cellars."

"So you're serious?" said Dagmar.

"Yeah. Is there a problem?"

"No problem at all," said Dagmar. "If you insist, you may certainly see the cellar."

"I insist," said McCobb.

Dagmar opened the cellar door and flipped on a light switch. "We'll follow you," she said.

McCobb walked carefully down the steps. The cellar was moist and slimy. It was lit by a naked lightbulb hanging from the ceiling. The strange coppery, earthy smell was much stronger down there than upstairs.

The sound he had heard upstairs was much louder down there, too: *Ch-ch-ch-ch-ch . . . Ch-ch-ch-ch-ch . . .* He wasn't surprised to see that the cellar floor had an inch of standing water. He was *extremely* surprised to see the several hundred slimy gray puppy-sized larvae in large cartons that completely covered the floor.

"What the heck are *those*?" he asked.

"I think you already know that," said Dagmar.

"I'm so dreadfully sorry you insisted on coming down here, dear," said Hedy.

Then they removed their big black hats. They removed their big black sunglasses. They lifted the bottoms of their pink rubber human masks, exposing their horrible black mandibles, and then they closed in on him.

Nobody but the Mandible sisters ever heard his screams.

CHAPTER 13

Old Friends Are the Best Friends

Special Agent Cromwell came out to the waiting room where the twins were sitting.

"Well, my investigator just called in," said Cromwell. "I've got to hand it to you kids. This is the best put-on I've ever gotten pulled on me. You really had me going there. Giant ants, right?" He laughed. "The best touch was getting Professor Spydelle to go along with it. How'd you ever get him to do that?"

"What?" said Wally.

"What are you talking about?" said Cheyenne.

"How did you ever talk Spydelle into going along with the gag?"

"What gag?" said Wally. "There isn't any gag."

"C'mon, son, it's over. You won. Enough is enough. My investigator just called me. He said there is no truth whatsoever to the allegation you and your sister made about the Mandible sisters."

"I don't understand," said Wally. "Maybe he just didn't look far enough. Maybe they didn't let him see the cellar."

"Son, my investigator is the best in the Bureau. It was a great gag, now let it go. Do you kids have a ride back home?"

"No," said Cheyenne. "Professor Spydelle drove us over here, but he's going to be working late."

"Well, just go down to the street and grab a cab," said Cromwell. He reached into his pocket, pulled out a pile of money, and peeled off a twenty-dollar bill. "This time of day, you shouldn't have any problem at all."

Down on the busy street, the cars sped by, and the cabs, when Wally and Cheyenne saw any, were always on the wrong side of the street. After trying unsuccessfully for an hour to get a cab to stop for them, they went back inside the FBI building.

"What do you think we ought to do?" asked Cheyenne. "Should we call the professor? Maybe he could leave work early and come get us."

"We don't really have a choice, do we?" said Wally.

A cab pulled up just outside the building.

"Wait! There's a cab!" shouted Cheyenne.

The twins rushed out of the building and opened the cab door, realizing too late that the cab was still occupied.

"Oh, excuse me," said Cheyenne. "I didn't realize there was anyone inside here."

"That's all right, dear," said a familiar voice. A surprisingly strong hand gripped her wrist and yanked her into the darkened cab.

At the same moment, another strong hand was gripping Wally's wrist and yanking him in as well.

The cab door was pulled shut.

Hedy and Dagmar welcomed the twins with open arms.

"You can't possibly know how glad we are to see you, my darlings," said Hedy.

CHAPTER 14

Pick One Destination and Stick to It!

The cab containing the Mandible sisters and the Shluffmuffin twins sped toward Dripping Fang Forest and certain doom for Wally and Cheyenne.

"Tell me exactly what you told the FBI about us," said Dagmar.

"It doesn't *matter* what they told the FBI about us, dear," said Hedy.

"It doesn't *matter*?" said Dagmar. "And why doesn't it matter, Hedy?"

"Because," said Hedy, "that investigator already filed his report. Before he had his unfortunate . . . accident." She giggled. "He said he found nothing suspicious. We *heard* him."

"It may not matter to *you*, Hedy," said Dagmar. "It happens to matter to *me*."

This may not be as bad as it looks, thought Cheyenne. *Dagmar seems to be madder at Hedy than she is at* us.

This is horrible, thought Wally. *This time we are really going to die. How could I have been so stupid? How could I have ever gotten into a cab without first looking to see if anybody was inside?*

The cab was headed across town, in the direction of the highway and the swamps.

I've got to get us out of here! thought Wally. *If I wait till we get to Dripping Fang Forest, it will be too late. If I throw myself at the door now and try to get it open, Dagmar and Hedy will stop me. They're much bigger than me and much stronger. And besides, jumping out of a moving cab will break every bone in our bodies. How can I get the cab to stop? How can I get us out of the cab if it stops?*

"I have to go to the bathroom," Wally announced. "I have to go pretty badly." He looked at Cheyenne.

"So do I," said Cheyenne. "*Really* badly."

"There'll be plenty of time for going to the bathroom when we get back to Mandible House, my dears," said Hedy.

"If I have to wait to go to the bathroom till we get all the way back to Mandible House," said Wally, "I'll go in my pants. It won't be too pleasant in here if I have to go in my pants, either. It's number two."

"If you insist on going in your pants, Walter, that's perfectly fine with *me*," said Dagmar.

"Yeah?" said the cab driver. "Well, lady, it sure ain't perfectly fine with *me*."

Dagmar sighed deeply. "Fine, driver. Pull up at the next gas station," she said. "Unlike you, I have all the time in the world."

"Driver," said Wally, "these women are kidnapping us. They're forcing us to go to their home against our will. Please take us to the nearest police station."

Cheyenne widened her eyes at him and shook her head.

"Okay, forget the police station," said Wally.

"Take us back to the FBI where you picked us up. Ask Special Agent Cromwell if we're telling the truth."

Cheyenne widened her eyes at him and shook her head.

"Okay, forget Agent Cromwell," said Wally. "Take us to the Museum of Natural History. Ask Professor Edgar Spydelle in the Bug Department if we're telling the truth."

"Driver," said Dagmar, "these children are runaways. We legally adopted them from the Jolly Days Orphanage, and they have run away from home. The police know all about them. If you want to drive us to a police station, that will be perfectly fine. We'll just have a much shorter ride, and you'll get a much smaller fare."

The driver jammed on his brakes, and the cab skidded to a shuddering stop. The driver turned around in his seat. He seemed pretty upset.

"Okay, folks, where we going?" he said. "First it's, 'Take us to Dripping Fang Forest.' Then it's, 'No, take us to a gas station.' Then it's,

'No, take us to a police station.' Then it's, 'No, take us to the FBI.' Then it's, 'No, take us to the Museum of Natural History.' I can't take any more of this. *Pick one destination and stick to it!* Otherwise, *get outta my cab*!"

"Good," said Wally. "I choose getting out of your cab."

He reached for the door handle. Dagmar grabbed his hand and squeezed so hard Wally heard crunching noises, and little pinpoints of light appeared in front of his eyes.

"Driver, we are going to Dripping Fang Forest, with a brief stop at the nearest service station," said Dagmar in a steely voice.

"Thank you so much," said the driver sarcastically. He turned back around and threw the cab in gear.

Ten minutes later, they pulled up at an Exxon station. Gripping him tightly and painfully by the wrist, Dagmar escorted Wally out of the cab and to the door of the men's room.

"You have exactly four minutes to do your business, Walter,"

Dagmar said. "I shall be waiting right outside, timing you." She shut the door.

Gripping Cheyenne tightly by her wrist, Hedy escorted Cheyenne to the ladies' room next door and let her go inside.

Once inside, Wally immediately locked the door. The men's room wasn't clean and it smelled like ammonia. People had written dumb things on the walls in bad handwriting. About waist high on one wall was a window with the glass painted over. Wally went to the window and tried to open it. The window was stuck, painted shut. He tried mightily to lift it, but he couldn't.

Wally's four minutes were slipping away. What could he do? He could smash the window, that's what he could do. But Dagmar would surely hear the sound, wouldn't she? Well, what if she did? Flushing the toilet to mask the sound, Wally shattered the window with his elbow.

"Walter, what was that noise?" Dagmar called out.

"What was *what* noise?" he answered.

"It sounded like glass breaking, Walter."

"Oh, *that* noise. I accidentally knocked a drinking glass off the sink."

Working swiftly, he carefully removed shards of glass from the window frame.

"Open the door, Walter!"

"But I'm not through pooping!"

"You are when I *say* you are!"

Dagmar pounded on the door. Wally boosted himself up onto the sill and climbed through the window frame.

"Walter, you open this door immediately, do you hear me?" shouted Dagmar.

Wally dropped to the grass in back of the gas station.

Outside the ladies' room, he tapped on the window.

"*Sssst*, Cheyenne!" he whispered. "Open the window!"

"Cheyenne, you open this door immediately!" cried Hedy.

Wally could hear Cheyenne struggling to get her window open. But it wouldn't budge more than an inch. He looked around for some kind of lever to force the window wider. He saw nothing. Then several yards away, he found a rusty old tire iron in the grass.

Dagmar kicked in the door of the men's room.

"Walter!" she shouted.

She rushed to the window and stuck her enormous head out.

"Walter, you get back here this instant, or I will do something extremely unpleasant to you!" she hissed.

"More unpleasant than killing me?" he said.

"*Much* more unpleasant than killing you!"

She put her huge foot up on the sill and began climbing through the window.

Wally jammed the tire iron under the stuck window of the ladies' room and forced it open.

"Cheyenne," he said, reaching through the window, "give me both your hands!"

Cheyenne reached up to Wally. He grabbed her by both hands and pulled. Cheyenne got both of her feet onto the window sill.

Because of her gigantic size, Dagmar was finding it difficult to fit herself through the men's room window frame. She stuck one leg out and then the other. She cut herself on the shards of glass and she swore loudly. Green liquid began to ooze out of her cuts.

"Jump, Cheyenne!" Wally shouted.

"Okay, here I come!" Cheyenne shouted.

Cheyenne jumped to the ground, sprawled in the grass, and scrambled to her feet.

In back of the gas station was a cornfield. The cornstalks—shiny green, succulent, and over six feet high—stood in rows so long you couldn't see the end of them.

"Now, *run!*" said Wally.

At last Dagmar got both feet on the ground and shouted for Hedy.

Cheyenne and Wally raced into the cornfield and began running down one of the narrow rows. Cornstalk leaves slapped their faces as they ran.

They were soon swallowed up by the corn-stalks.

"We did it!" shouted Cheyenne happily, puffing hard as she ran. "We got away from them again!"

"This time *we* were the lucky ones," said Wally. "Next time I'm afraid it'll be *them*."

What's Next for the Shluffmuffin Twins?

Have Wally and Cheyenne truly escaped the clutches of the gruesome Mandible sisters, or will they be recaptured on the other side of that cornfield?

How long can the twins pretend to prefer Professor Spydelle and his enormous, hairy eight-legged spider wife, when they secretly yearn to be reunited with their beloved but still dead father? How long can Vampire Dad restrain himself from forcibly taking his children back from the Spydelles or, for that matter, from biting their necks? Can you be both a blood-sucking creature of the night and a responsible, loving father?

Can the Mandible sisters succeed in infecting an entire city with flu virus and harvest enough snot to feed the super-larvae? Can they succeed in breeding a race of super-ants to replace mankind and end life on Earth as we know it? What would life on Earth as we know it be like if it were no longer as we knew it, and how would we know that?

You seriously can*not* afford to miss the Shluff-muffins' next pulse-pounding, heart-stopping, hysteria-inducing adventure—Secrets of Dripping Fang, Book Four: *Fall of the House of Mandible*!

DAN GREENBURG writes the popular Zack Files series for kids and has also written many bestselling books for grown-ups. His sixty-six books have been translated into twenty languages. To research his writing, Dan has worked with N.Y. firefighters and homicide cops, searched for the Loch Ness monster, flown upside down in an open-cockpit plane, taken part in voodoo ceremonies in Haiti, and disciplined tigers on a Texas ranch. He has not, however, personally encountered any zombies or vampires—at least not yet. Dan lives north of New York with wife Judith, son Zack, and many cats.

SCOTT M. FISCHER glided through high school doing extra-credit art assignments for math teachers, which is kinda boring stuff to draw. Next he went to art school, where he learned to paint even more boring things—like flower vases. However, he swears that since then he has drawn nothing but cool stuff—like oozy, drooling monsters, treacherous villains, and the occasional flower vase . . . that has fangs and eats flowers for breakfast!